# The Winged Tiger

## and

# The Dragons of Hawaii

## by Phil Yeh and Jon J. Murakami

Color and layout by Lieve Jerger

First Edition. 2004

**Other books by Phil Yeh:**

Cazco 1976

Jam 1977 with Don DeContreras, Roberta Gregory and friends

Even Cazco Gets the Blues 1977

Ajaneh 1978

Godiva 1979

Cazco in China 1980

The Adventures of a Modern Day Unicorn 1981 starring Frank the Unicorn

Frank on the Farm 1982 illustrated introduction by Sergio Aragones

Mr. Frank Goes to Washington, D.C. 1984

Frank & Syd on The Brooklyn Bridge 1986 with Dennis Niedbala

Frank in England 1987

The Penguin is Mightier Than the Swordfish 1987 with Leigh Rubin

The Frank the Unicorn comic book series since 1986

The Penguin and Pencilguin comic book series since 1987

The Patrick Rabbit comic book series since 1988

Theo the Dinosaur 1991

The Winged Tiger graphic novel 1993. Illustrated Introductions by Jean "Moebius" Giraud and Wendy Pini

Voyage to Veggie Isle 1993

The Winged Tiger's World Peace Party Puzzle Book 1997

The Winged Tiger & The Lace Princess 1998 with Lieve Jerger

The Winged Tiger comic book series since 1998

**Other books by Jon J. Murakami:**

Written by Peter Coraggio and illustrated by Jon J. Murakami:

The Art of Piano Performance: Pedaling - The Soul of the Piano: Introducing the Pedals and Basic Pedaling -1996

The Art of Piano Performance: The Spectrum of Expressive Touches -1997

The Art of Piano Performance: Perfect Practice -or- Chunks, Clumps, Hunks, Clods, Blocks, Slivers, Slices, and Globs -1997

The Art of Piano Performance: Imagery in Music: Italian Terms of Tempo, Character, and Spirit -2000

The Art of Piano Performance: Musical Style - Introduction to the Baroque, Classical, and Romantic Eras -2003

The Winged Tiger and The Dragons of Hawaii

First Edition. Summer 2004 published by Eastwind Studios, est. 1970, P. O. Box 670, Lompoc, California 93438 USA

**www.wingedtiger.com**

Printed in Hong Kong

ISBN 0-9755635-0-5

Once upon a time during the Dark Ages, when people were not very bright...

there lived a little dragon called Red

and a little mouse called Fred, who said:
"Hey, this is the Dark Ages, turn out the light!"

Fred and Red were actually friends, although Fred had a rather bad temper. They lived in an old castle and every day, Fred got up on the wrong side of the bed.

Red tried to get Fred to move his bed from the edge of the castle wall but Fred was very stubborn. Fred liked to do things his own way even if it was the wrong way.

Red loved to play his saxophone and he tried to encourage Fred to play the harmonica, but Fred wanted to play the tuba instead.

Red said: "The tuba is too big for you, Fred. Why not try the triangle?" But Fred just got mad and said that he was never going to play music again. Red continued to practice his sax and, in time, became the most famous sax player in the kingdom.

One day an armadillo knight in shining armor stopped by the castle to deliver an invitation for Red to come and play his sax for the King's birthday party.

So Fred and Red headed off to the King's castle on the day of the birthday. Fred insisted on coming along to protect Red from any danger. As they crossed a bridge, a big troll stopped them and demanded their money to cross the bridge.

Since Red and Fred didn't have any money, they decided to make a run for it. Fred ran into a little mouse hole and Red ran into a cave — a very small cave that had no another way out. The troll waited outside the cave for Red to come out.

Just then, The Winged Tiger, who was more often seen in the days of castles, appeared in the cave with a magic hoop.
Red jumped through the hoop and was gone!

Meanwhile in Asia, another dragon named Erin
was going to a kite festival to play her flute.

When Erin arrived at the kite festival, all the kites were gone. She asked a little rabbit what had happened to the kites. "A rich panda bought them all," said the little rabbit. "But how can we have a festival without any kites?" said Erin. "I don't know" said the rabbit, "but we bought some bamboo-shoot candy with the money he gave us."

Erin noticed that most of the people were going home. There wasn't much of a kite-flying festival without any kites. Erin had been practicing her flute for months for this day, and now it looked like there would be no audience to hear her perform.

Suddenly she heard a cry for help. It was the rich panda.
He had bought all the kites and now they were carrying him up into the sky.

Erin flew up to save the rich panda. She took kites from his hand and gently put him back on the ground. The panda promised never to be greedy again. He asked Erin to return the kites to their owners.

Suddenly, a strong gust of wind blew Erin into a big storm cloud.

There was lightning and thunder all around poor Erin.
She worried that a lightning bolt might strike her and her flute.

Just in the nick of time, The Winged Tiger appeared with another magical hoop. Erin dove through the hoop and was gone. The Winged Tiger returned all the kites to the kids below and they all decided to go home since the festival was rained out.

Meanwhile, far in outer space, on an asteroid filled with old junk,
a dragon called Rusty was playing his keyboards.

The asteroid attracted junk-eating robots from all over the galaxy.
It was hard for Rusty to find peace and quiet to practice on his keyboards.

Rusty tried to get the robots to eat healthier and quieter foods,
but the robots liked eating junk. The junk tasted good.

Rusty decided to go and find a quiet place to practice.
He flew to the other side of the asteroid, where he saw a big hill.

"This is perfect," said Rusty, "Now I can play my keyboards in peace."

Rusty didn't realize that he was not on a big hill. He was actually on the head of a giant robot. The giant was making a sandwich out of some junk and he thought a little dragon and a keyboard would taste great.

The giant robot reached up and grabbed Rusty and his keyboard.
Rusty thought that he had played his last note.

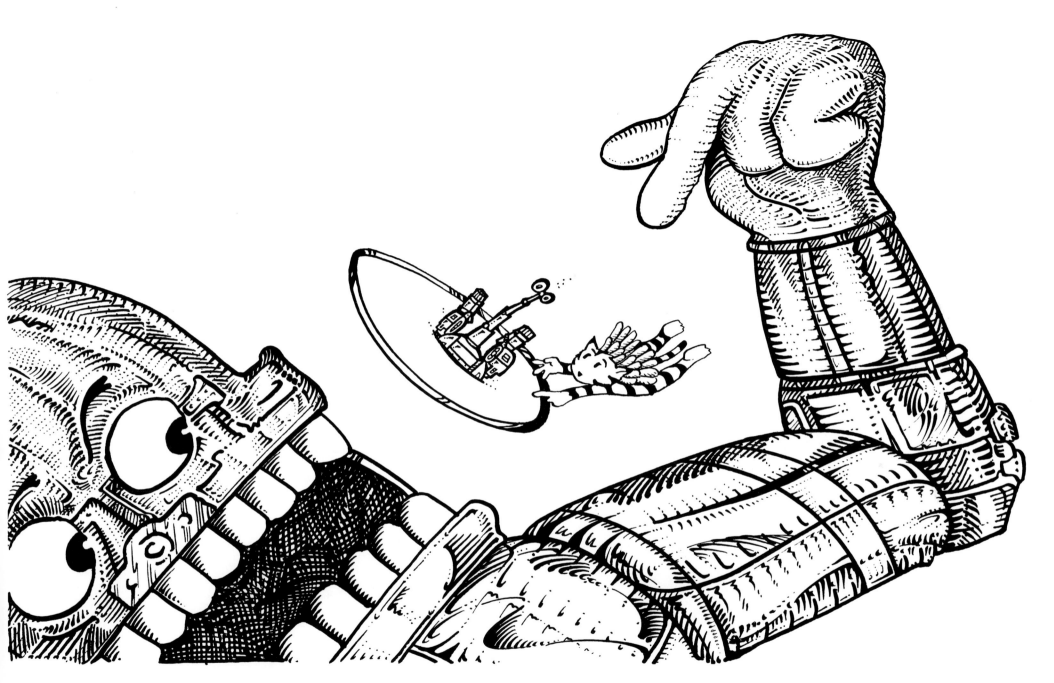

What a shock! The Winged Tiger appeared out of the sky with his magical hoop, just as Rusty was on his way to becoming a snack.

Meanwhile, in a city undersea, lived a water dragon named Lilly. She loved to play her violin. She practiced all the time and soon everyone came to hear her play.

Urchie the sea urchin did not like the fact that everyone enjoyed Lilly's violin playing. She was very jealous of Lilly. She wanted everyone to like her instead of Lilly.

When Lilly went to sit down and practice some new music,
Urchie jumped on the stool and surprised her.

One day, Lilly went to play for the birthday celebration of the Mermaid Princess.
The Princess had arranged to have Lilly play on a horse-float in a lagoon.

Lilly didn't know that Urchie was hiding under the horse-float with another one of her surprises.

Pop! One little touch from Urchie and the air started shooting
out of the float, sending it into the sky with Lilly!

Right towards the birthday cake
made especially for the Mermaid Princess.

By now you know that this was the exact perfect moment for The Winged Tiger and his magical hoop to appear right in front of the cake.

Meanwhile in a tropical jungle, a dragon called Geo was actually at work playing his drums. He sent messages from everyone in the jungle to their friends by beating his drums. His friend Slim The Sloth was always hanging around Geo. He thought that he could play the drums as well as Geo.

Slim told Geo that he could handle the drum message service,
while Geo took a vacation. Geo told Slim that he had to make sure
that he did a good job and didn't miss any messages.

After Geo left on his trip, Slim heard two lizards named Tee and Vee talking about a boxing match they were going to have inside a box. Slim loved to watch fights so he went down to check it out.

Tee and Vee were both good boxers and the match went on and on.
Slim became tired from watching Tee and Vee so he went to sleep.
After all, he was a sloth and he had to sleep a lot.

Slim The Sloth slept for the next week. The messages didn't get sent out and they didn't get recorded when they came in. Everyone in the jungle was worried that something had happened to the drums.

Finally, Geo came back from his vacation only to find his boss with a brand-new telephone to replace his drums. Geo was fired, thanks to Slim sleeping on the job.

Geo wasn't stuck in the jungle for very long. The Winged Tiger showed up with his magical hoop to take Geo away.

This time, The Winged Tiger also flew through the hoop.

Now you are probably wondering who The Winged Tiger is and what he was
doing with these magical hoops. Well, the legends all say that The Winged Tiger
often appears in people's lives just when we need to make a change.
He has been seen all over the world,  in the strangest places.

These five dragons from five very different places all have one thing in common: they love to play music and want to live in a place where they can play in peace. Thanks to The Winged Tiger's magical hoops, their dreams have come true.

A long time ago, these five dragons became known as

*The Dragons of Hawaii.*

Some day, if you are very lucky, you might hear their music
while on a beach in a place that many people call "paradise."
Or you may even read about their fine adventures
in other parts of the world.

But that's another story, for another time.
Aloha!